KT-513-239

The Magic Pyjamas

by Karen Wallace and
Manola Caprini

W
FRANKLIN WATTS
LONDON•SYDNEY

Franklin Watts

First published in Great Britain in 2016 by
The Watts Publishing Group

Text © Karen Wallace 2016
Illustrations © Manola Caprini 2016

Series Editor: Jackie Hamley
Series Advisor: Catherine Glavina
Series Designer: Peter Scoulding

A CIP catalogue record for this book is available
from the British Library.

ISBN 978 1 4451 4596 9 hbk)
ISBN 978 1 4451 4589 1 (pbk)
ISBN 978 1 4451 4590 7 (library ebook)

Printed in China

Franklin Watts
An imprint of
Hachette Children's Group
Part of The Watts Publishing Group
Carmelite House
50 Victoria Embankment
London EC4Y 0DZ

An Hachette UK company.
www.hachette.co.uk

www.franklinwatts.co.uk

For Seren and Alys
– K.W.

Jack was a boy who could not go to sleep.

3

He tried counting sheep
but that was too difficult.

He tried writing, "I will go to sleep!" one hundred times.

But he ran out of paper.

Mum gave him a parrot that said: "Go to sleep! Go to sleep!"

But it flew out the window.

"Why can't you sleep?" asked Dad.

"Sleeping is boring," said Jack. "Nothing ever happens."

No one in the family knew
what to do.

13

One day, a parcel arrived.
The note said: "Dear Jack,
These are magic pyjamas.
Love, Granny."

15

Jack put on the pyjamas and got into bed.

"Nothing magic here," he said. He lay down.

17

Jack roared off in a plane and landed on a mountain by the sea.

VROOM!

19

He ran down to the shore and built himself a tree house.

21

Hundreds of birds flew by
and he counted each one.

Jack's head was full of amazing pictures.

He yawned and closed
his eyes.

"There's no such thing as magic pyjamas," said Dad. "I know," said Mum.

They looked into Jack's
bedroom.

The star on his pyjamas glowed in the dark. Jack was asleep!

29

Puzzle 1

Put these pictures in the correct order.
Now tell the story in your own words.
Can you think of a different ending?

Puzzle 2

bored   cheerful

disinterested

furious   calm

peaceful

Choose the words which best describe
Jack at the beginning and end of the story.
Can you think of any more?

Answers

Puzzle 1

The correct order is:

1d, 2e, 3a, 4c, 5f, 6b

Puzzle 2

Beginning   The correct words are bored, disinterested.

The incorrect word is cheerful.

End   The correct words are calm, peaceful.

The incorrect word is furious.

Look out for more stories:

Bill's Silly Hat
ISBN 978 1 4451 1617 4

Little Joe's Boat Race
ISBN 978 0 7496 9467 8

Little Joe's Horse Race
ISBN 978 1 4451 1619 8

Felix, Puss in Boots
ISBN 978 1 4451 1621 1

Cheeky Monkey's Big Race
ISBN 978 1 4451 1618 1

The Animals' Football Cup
ISBN 978 0 7496 9477 7

The Animals' Football Camp
ISBN 978 1 4451 1616 7

The Animals' Football Final
ISBN 978 1 4451 3879 4

That Noise!
ISBN 978 0 7496 9479 1

The Frog Prince and the Kitten
ISBN 978 1 4451 1620 4

Gerald's Busy Day
ISBN 978 1 4451 3939 5

Dani's Dinosaur
ISBN 978 1 4451 3945 6

The Cowboy Kid
ISBN 978 1 4451 3949 4

Robbie's Robot
ISBN 978 1 4451 3953 1

The Green Machines
ISBN 978 1 4451 3957 9

For details of all our titles go to: www.franklinwatts.co.uk